Dear Parent:
Your child's love of reading starts here!

Every child learns to read in a different way and at his or her own speed. Some go back and forth between reading levels and read favorite books again and again. Others read through each level in order. You can help your young reader improve and become more confident by encouraging his or her own interests and abilities. From books your child reads with you to the first books he or she reads alone, there are I Can Read Books for every stage of reading:

SHARED READING
Basic language, word repetition, and whimsical illustrations, ideal for sharing with your emergent reader

BEGINNING READING
Short sentences, familiar words, and simple concepts for children eager to read on their own

READING WITH HELP
Engaging stories, longer sentences, and language play for developing readers

READING ALONE
Complex plots, challenging vocabulary, and high-interest topics for the independent reader

ADVANCED READING
Short paragraphs, chapters, and exciting themes for the perfect bridge to chapter books

I Can Read Books have introduced children to the joy of reading since 1957. Featuring award-winning authors and illustrators and a fabulous cast of beloved characters, I Can Read Books set the standard for beginning readers.

A lifetime of discovery begins with the magical words "I Can Read!"

Visit www.icanread.com for information
on enriching your child's reading experience.

The Berenstain Bears: We Love Trucks! Copyright © 2013 by Berenstain Publishing, Inc. All rights reserved. Manufactured in China. No part of this book may be used or reproduced in any manner whatsoever without written permission except in the case of brief quotations embodied in critical articles and reviews. For information address HarperCollins Children's Books, a division of HarperCollins Publishers, 10 East 53rd Street, New York, NY 10022.
www.icanread.com

Library of Congress catalog card number: 201294167
ISBN 978-0-06-207536-9 (trade bdg.)—ISBN 978-0-06-207535-2 (pbk.)

12 13 14 15 16   SCP   10 9 8 7 6 5 4 3 2 1

❖

First Edition

I Can Read!

BEGINNING READING 1

The Berenstain Bears®
WE ♥ TRUCKS!

Jan & Mike Berenstain

HARPER
An Imprint of HarperCollinsPublishers

Grizzly Gramps drives a pickup truck.

He is driving it to Farmer Ben's farm.

He needs to pick up things at the farm.

Brother, Sister, and Honey Bear are going with him.

They love Gramps's pickup truck.

"You cubs like trucks, right?"
asks Gramps.

"Yes!" they say.

"We will see lots of trucks on our way,"

says Gramps.

"Yay!" say the cubs.

7

"Hiya, Joe!" calls Gramps.

"How are the flowers today?"

"Nice and fresh!" calls Joe.

"Any letters for me, Herb?" asks Gramps.

"Not today, Gramps," says Herb.

They see builders at work.

"Hey, Gus!" calls Gramps. "Can we see your dump truck?"

"Sure!" says Gus.

DUMP TRUCK

Gramps and the cubs get into
the dump truck. It is huge!
Gus dumps a big load of dirt out the back.
"Wow!" say the cubs.

They pass more trucks.

"They're on the way to the hospital,"
says Gramps.

"It's loud!" says Sister, holding her ears.

AMBULANCE

BEAR COUNTRY RESCUE

A tow truck is towing a car.

"Careful, Jane!" calls Gramps.

"Don't scratch it!"

TOW TRUCK

JANE'S TOWING

MAYOR

STOP

13

They come to a firehouse.

The fire trucks are parked outside.

The firefighters are practicing.

PUMPER FIRE TRUCK

Gramps and the cubs stop to watch.

The firefighters squirt water from a hose.

They climb up a big ladder.

HOOK-AND-LADDER
FIRE TRUCK

15

Gramps and the cubs pass bears
picking up the trash.

GARBAGE TRUCK

They pass bears pouring cement
for a sidewalk.

CEMENT MIXER

"Someone is moving in here,"
says Gramps, stopping.
He shakes hands with
the new family.

"Welcome to the neighborhood!" he says.

MOVING VAN

19

Gramps drives on.

They pass a car sale lot.

Bears are unloading cars.

CAR CARRIER

NEW CARS

"Be careful, boys!" calls Gramps.

"Don't drop any of 'em!"

Gramps stops at a gas station.

Bears are at work pumping gas.

They pump it into big tanks
in the ground.

FUEL TRUCK

Out on the highway, they pass
a really big truck.

TRACTOR-TRAILER TRUCK

The cubs ask the driver
to blow his horn.

"*HONNNK!*" goes the horn.

Gramps visits his friends the Browns.

They are getting ready for a trip.

They are going in a big truck.

RV

It is like a house on wheels.

The cubs go in. It is nice inside.

They even have TV!

Back on the road,

they pass a line of trucks.

Soldiers are on the trucks.

They are from the army.

ARMY TRUCKS

Gramps and the cubs salute.

The soldiers salute back!

Finally, Gramps comes to
Farmer Ben's farm.
Gramps loads baskets of fruit
into his truck.

Farmer Ben is going to a farm show.

He is putting his donkey into his truck.

The donkey doesn't want to go!

"Good luck, Ben!" calls Gramps.

HORSE TRAILER

Gramps drives back to the tree house.

Lizzy and Barry Bruin are visiting.

"Bye, cubs!" says Gramps.

"Bye, Gramps!" say the cubs. "We had fun!"

"Bye-bye, little truck!" says little Honey.

MINIVAN